How I Spent My Summer Vacation

written and illustrated by Mark Teague

Scholastic Inc.   New York Toronto London Auckland Sydney

For Rebecca and Jerry and Mark

ISBN 0-590-97516-1

Copyright © 1995 by Mark Teague.
All rights reserved. Published by Scholastic Inc., 555 Broadway, New York, NY 10012, by arrangement with Crown Publishers, Inc., a Random House Company.

12 11 10 9 8 7 6 5 4 3 2 1   6 7 8 9/9 0 1/0

Printed in the U.S.A.   08

First Scholastic printing, September 1996

When summer began, I headed out west.

My parents had told me I needed a rest.

"Your imagination," they said, "is getting too wild.

It will do you some good to relax for a while."

So they put me aboard a westbound train

To visit Aunt Fern in her house on the plains.

But I was captured by cowboys,
A wild-looking crowd.
Their manners were rough
and their voices were loud.

"I'm trying to get to my aunt's house," I said.
But they carried me off to their cow camp instead.

The Cattle Boss growled, as he told me to sit,
"We need a new cowboy. Our old cowboy quit.
We could sure use your help. So what do you say?"
I thought for a minute, then I told him, "Okay."

Then I wrote to Aunt Fern, so she'd know where I'd gone.
I said not to worry, I wouldn't be long.

Dear Aunt,
Captured by
Cowboys. Don't
Worry. See
You soon.
Love,
Wallace

Aunt Fern
P.O. Box 5
Prairie
Tumblewe

19¢

That night I was given a new set of clothes.

Soon I looked like a wrangler from my head to my toes.

But there's more to a cowboy than boots and a hat,

I found out the next day

And the day after that.

Each day I discovered some new cowboy tricks.

From roping

And riding

To making fire with sticks.

Slowly the word spread all over the land:

"That wrangler 'Kid Bleff' is a first-rate cowhand!"

The day finally came when the roundup was through.
Aunt Fern called: "Come on over. Bring your cowboys with you."

She was cooking a barbecue that very same day.
So we cleaned up (a little) and we headed her way.

The food was delicious. There was plenty to eat.
And the band that was playing just couldn't be beat.

But suddenly I noticed a terrible sight.
The cattle were stirring and stamping with fright.
It's a scene I'll remember till my very last day.
"They're gonna stampede!" I heard somebody say.

Just then they came charging. They charged right at *me!*
I looked for a hiding place—
a rock, or a tree.

What I found was a tablecloth spread out on the ground.

So I turned like a matador

And spun it around.

It was a new kind of cowboying, a fantastic display!

The cattle were frightened and stampeded . . . away!

Then the cowboys all cheered, "Bleff's a true buckaroo!"

They shook my hand and slapped my back,

And Aunt Fern hugged me, too.

And *that's* how I spent my summer vacation.

I can hardly wait for show-and-tell!